Written by
James Gelsey

D0001786

WORLDWIDE PUBLISHING

A
LITTLE APPLE
PAPERBACK

SCHOLASTIC INC.

New York   Toronto   London   Auckland   Sydney
Mexico City   New Delhi   Hong Kong

ISBN 0-590-81909-7

40 39 38 37 36 35 34 33   8 9/0

Special thanks to Arkadia for interior illustrations.

Printed in the U.S.A.

First Scholastic printing, November 1998

For Sue

Chapter 1

B *OOM!* The thunder rumbled through the dark, stormy night.

"Yikes! What was that?" asked Shaggy from the back of the Mystery Machine.

"Just a little thunder, Shaggy. Nothing to be worried about," Daphne said from the front seat.

"Nothing to be worried about? Didja hear that, Scoob? The sky's gonna come crashing down on us at any minute and there's nothing to be worried about."

1

"Come on, Shaggy," Fred called from the driver's seat. "We'll make it to the movie just fine. It's only a little storm."

"I hope you're right, man, 'cause I'm getting hungry. How 'bout you, Scooby-Doo?"

"Rou bet!" Scooby said, wagging his tail.

The Mystery Machine carefully made its way along the winding roads. It was raining hard, but the movie theater was just a few miles away.

"Jinkies," Velma said. "Fred, maybe this wasn't such a great shortcut."

"Yeah, it seems really dark," Daphne added. "Can you see the road okay?"

"I can see it just fine," Fred answered.

BANG!

The Mystery Machine hit a huge bump and suddenly skidded off the road.

"The sky is falling!" Shaggy yelled.

"Rold me, Raggy!" Scooby jumped into Shaggy's arms.

The van came to a stop.

"Is everyone okay?" Fred asked.

"I'm fine," Daphne said. "Velma?"

"I'm okay, thanks. Good thing I was wearing my seat belt," she added.

Fred turned around toward the back. "How about you guys?"

Shaggy and Scooby were nowhere to be seen.

"Shaggy? Scooby-Doo?" Velma said.

"We're fine," came Shaggy's voice from under the rear seat. "We're just, like, uh, checking to make sure the floor's okay."

"Hmmm . . ." Daphne said. "I wonder what happened."

"Judging by the sound, I'll bet it's a flat," Velma said.

"I'll check it out," Fred said. He grabbed a flashlight from the glove compartment and went out to look at the tires.

"You can come out now, fellas," Velma said. "I'm sure the floor is fine."

"You can never be too sure, right, Scoob?" Shaggy said.

"Right!" Scooby barked.

Fred got back into the van. "It's a flat, all right. We must've hit a rock or something back there. Everyone sit tight. We'll be on our way to the movie before you know it. Shaggy, give me a hand with the spare."

"Uh, no can do, Freddy-o," Shaggy said.

"Why not?" Fred asked. "Don't tell me you're still scared of the storm."

"I'm not scared of the storm," Shaggy replied.

BOOOOOM!

"Yikes! The sky's falling again!" Shaggy

yelled. He jumped into Scooby's arms. Scooby started laughing. Velma, Daphne, and Fred did, too.

"Like, what's so funny?" Scooby looked at Shaggy and said, *"BOOOOOM!"* Everyone started laughing again.

"Very funny, Scooby-Doo," Shaggy said.

"Enough kidding around," Fred said. "Let's get this tire changed."

"Like I said before, Fred, no can do. There's no spare."

"No spare?" Fred, Daphne, and Velma all looked at one another. Then they looked at Shaggy and Scooby. "Why not?"

"Like, Scooby and I needed room for our emergency survival kit. It contains every-thing we need to survive an emergency. Right, Scooby?"

Scooby shook his head up and down.

5

"I'm afraid to see this survival kit," Daphne said.

"I have a pretty good hunch what's inside," Velma added.

Shaggy opened the spare tire compartment. Inside were cookies, chips, cakes, soda pop, and submarine sandwiches.

"Well, gang, we're stuck in a storm with a flat and no spare tire," Fred said.

"Sounds like an emergency situation to me," Shaggy said.

"Me roo!" Scooby agreed. The two of them reached for some snacks and started eating.

"Hey! What's that?" Daphne said. She pointed through the windshield. Lightning flashed across the sky

again. It lit up the outline of a huge castle just up the road. "It looks like a house," she said.

"More like a mansion," Fred added.

6

"More like a castle," Velma said.

"More like a haunted castle, if you ask me," Shaggy said.

"There's only one thing to do," Fred said. "Let's go get help."

"We can use their phone," Velma said. "Then maybe we can still make the movie."

Shaggy and Scooby didn't budge.

"Aren't you coming, boys?" Daphne asked.

"No, thank you," Shaggy said, shaking his head. "Going to a big scary castle on a stormy night spells nothing but trouble."

"Nothing but rouble!" Scooby echoed.

"You're being ridiculous. That castle isn't haunted," Velma said.

Shaggy took a bite out of his sandwich. "We'll be fine right here."

"Suit yourself," Fred said.

Shaggy and Scooby watched their friends get out of the van. Velma led the way, shining the flashlight through the rain. After a moment or two, they were gone.

"They're outside in the pouring rain. We're inside a dry van with our emergency survival kit. Who's ridiculous now, huh, Scooby?"

FLASH! CRASH! BOOM! Shaggy and Scooby watched a lightning bolt strike a tree next to the Mystery Machine. The tree crashed to the ground. The whole Mystery Machine shook. Shaggy and Scooby looked at each other.

"WAIT FOR US!"

They jumped out of the van and raced toward the castle.

Chapter 2

Shaggy and Scooby ran up the winding driveway toward Montgomery Castle. The road was very steep, and the pouring rain didn't make the climb any easier. Finally, Shaggy and Scooby managed to reach the top. They arrived at the front door out of breath.

"So, like, I wonder where Fred and the girls are," Shaggy said, looking around.

"Boo!"

Shaggy and Scooby screamed.

It was only Fred. He was standing there

with Daphne and Velma. "We thought that was you running past us." Fred laughed.

"So, Shaggy," Daphne said, "why'd you leave the safety of the van?"

"Like, the van wasn't so safe anymore," Shaggy said.

"Rim-ber!" Scooby shouted. He fell over like a tree into Shaggy's arms.

"Enough clowning around. We're here to use the phone," Fred said. He reached for the door knocker. "I just hope somebody's home," he added.

"Judging by the lights up there, I'd say there's a good chance," Velma offered. She pointed to the large windows on the second floor.

The door slowly creaked open. The gang looked inside but couldn't see a thing. Then, out of the darkness a face appeared. It was

the face of an old, old man. The candle he
was holding gave his face an eerie glow.

"Uh, Scooby-Doo and I just remembered
we forgot to do something," Shaggy said.

"What's that?" asked Daphne.

"Stay in the van!" Shaggy replied.

"Please," the old man said. He placed his
wrinkled hand on Shaggy's shoulder. "Please,
come in."

Shaggy gulped. "Nothing to be afraid of,
Scooby," Shaggy said. "You go first." He gave

Scooby a push. The gang followed Scooby through the doorway and into the dark front hall. The door closed behind them with a slam.

"My name is Chives," the elderly man said.

"Pardon me," Fred said, "but our van has a flat tire out in front of your house and —"

"Well, Chives, who's here?" asked a strange voice. Another man approached. He was also carrying a candle. "The name's Clifton Montgomery. This is my butler, Chives. Frightful night, isn't it?"

"Yes, it is, Mr. Montgomery," Fred replied.

"Please, call me Clift. Do come in and dry off," Clift continued. "I'm so sorry about the lights. The fixture is under repair and we never got around to putting any candles here."

"Excuse me, Mr. Montgomery, but —" Fred started to say.

"Uh-uh-uh — call me Clift."

"Okay, Clift. Can we use your phone? Our van out front has a flat and we don't have a spare." Fred glared at Shaggy and Scooby. "So sorry, but the phone lines are down. Chives will take care of it once the storm passes. Now please, join us for dinner."

"That's very generous, Clift, but —" Velma began.

"I won't take no for an answer," interrupted Clift.

13

Shaggy and Scooby looked at each other. "You heard the man. He won't take no for an answer. Maybe this place isn't so bad, after all," Shaggy said.

Chives led the way out of the front hall and up a huge, curving staircase. As the gang made their way up, Scooby and Shaggy sniffed the air. Their keen sense of smell caught a whiff of fresh roast beef.

"Like I said be-fore, Scooby-Doo," Shaggy said, "there's nothing to be afraid of here."

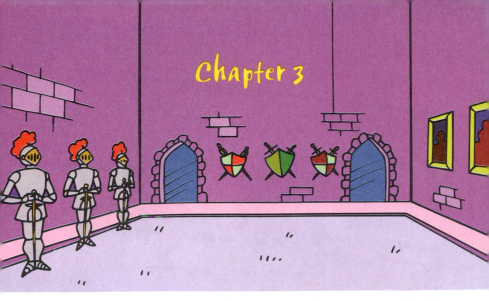

Chapter 3

At the top of the stairs, the gang found themselves in the Great Hall. It was the largest room they had ever seen in a house of any size. Everything about it was big. The walls seemed fifty feet high and were made of huge blocks of stone. An assortment of old shields, swords, and other medieval tools covered one wall. A row of ten suits of armor, each seven feet high, lined another wall. Above, they noticed three giant candelabras glowing with the light of a hundred candles.

"Jinkies, who's that?" Velma asked. She

15

pointed to a huge painting of a man. He looked very stern.

"That's Ward Montgomery, my great-great-grandfather," Clift said.

"Amazing," Daphne said.

"Wow," Fred added.

"So, like, when do we eat?" asked Shaggy.

Chives walked up behind Shaggy. "Right this way, sir," he said.

Shaggy jumped. "Like, don't sneak up on us like that, man," Shaggy said. "You almost scared poor Scooby to death. You okay, Scoob? Scoob?" Shaggy looked around but Scooby wasn't there. Scooby was already following the aroma of roast beef.

"Your dog would make a fine bloodhound," Clift said. "He's already found his way to the dining room. Shall we?" Clift motioned for everyone to follow Scooby-Doo.

The dining room was brightly lit by several electric chandeliers. There were already a few people sitting around the long table, but Shaggy and Scooby-Doo didn't notice the people. They were looking at all the food.

"Now this is what I call a dinner table," Shaggy said in awe. Down the center of the long table was a row of silver platters. Each platter was piled high with food.

"Do you see what I see, Scooby?" Shaggy asked.

"Rou bet," Scooby replied.

The two of them walked over to the table. Never before had they seen so much food. There was roast beef, chicken, fish, vegetables of all kinds, long breads, skinny breads, round breads, and platters with mounds of spaghetti.

"Please, please, have a seat anywhere," Clift said. He waved his hand and pointed to some empty chairs. The gang sat down around the table.

"I have some very exciting news to share," Clift said from the head of the table. "But before I start, let's take a moment to introduce ourselves. It's so much nicer eating with friends than strangers."

"Really, Clift, is this another of your silly games?" asked the woman sitting next to him.

Fred shrugged and said, "I guess I'll start. I'm Fred, and this is Daphne, Velma, Shaggy, and Scooby-Doo. Our van has a flat just outside the castle. We only came in to use the phone."

"And I forced them to join us for dinner. The more the merrier, I always say. Barbara, your turn."

"I'm Barbara Redding," said the woman sitting next to Clift. "You probably already know that I'm the mayor of this town. And I've been trying to convince Clift to donate the castle to the town as a museum."

The old man next to Velma leaned forward in his chair and coughed. "Sonny DiPesto. Real estate, shopping malls, parking garages. I've been after this place for years

for a medieval-themed amusement park. I want to call it Knightland."

The woman with red hair across from him shook her head disapprovingly. "I'm Sally MacIntyre, from Scotland's Royal Museum. We've been trying to get this castle returned to Scotland where it belongs."

Clift stood beside his chair at the head of the table. "Now, some of you may not know the rich history of the Montgomery family. How my great-great-grandfather, Ward Montgomery, brought this castle over from Scotland stone by stone. The Montgomery family has lived here for years. And as you may know, I have no family of my own. Therefore, as of midnight tonight, I am turning the castle over to the people of our town for use as a museum and park."

Mayor Redding jumped out of her chair. "How wonderful!" she exclaimed.

Sonny DiPesto reached for his water glass. "We'll see how long a museum lasts in this town," he muttered under his breath.

"Ah, 'tis a sad, sad day for the folks back in Scotland," Sally said to Daphne.

"A toast to Clifton Montgomery," Mayor Redding said. Everyone raised their glasses.

"I love a good toast," Shaggy said, "especially with butter and jam."

"Rike ris!" Scooby took a huge bite of bread and smiled.

"Hip, hip, hooray!" everyone cheered. "Hip, hip, hooray!"

And suddenly, the lights went out.

Chapter 4

"Like, where is everybody?" Shaggy asked.

"Everyone stay calm," Clift called. "Just a temporary power failure. Chives will get some candles. Chives!"

Someone struck a match. A candle was lit in the darkness. It slowly moved and illuminated a ghostly face.

"It looks like Ward Montgomery!" Velma cried.

The ghost's face was pale. His skin looked wrinkled and saggy. There was no mistaking it. It was Ward Montgomery!

"Like, I told you guys this place was haunted!" Shaggy said.

The ghost began to speak in a scratchy voice. "Montgomery Castle must remain in our family. I curse every stone in this castle and anyone who dares to remain here after midnight. Leave this place now and never return. Let what happens to my great-great-grandson be your only warning."

The ghost blew out the candle.

Suddenly, Clift screamed. Then there was the sound of a door slamming.

"What's going on?" Mayor Redding yelled.

A moment later, the lights came back on. Clift was gone. Everyone called for him but he did not answer. Shaggy looked over and saw that Scooby-Doo was also gone.

"Oh, no! The ghost got Scooby-Doo, too. Scoob? Scooby-Doo, where are you?" he called.

"Runder rere," Scooby's voice came from under the table.

Shaggy lifted the tablecloth. There was Scooby under the table. He had a big platter of spaghetti in front of him.

"That's the spirit, Scooby. No sense being scared on an empty stomach." Shaggy then joined him under the table.

"Sonny," Mayor Redding said, "what are you doing over there?"

Sonny was standing by the large grandfather clock, holding a candle. "After the ghost blew out the candle, I heard some sounds come from over here," Sonny explained. "I moved as fast as I could, but by the time I got here, all I could find was this candle."

"We'd better get some help," the mayor decided. "With the phone lines out, we'll have to drive back to town." Mayor Redding, Sonny DiPesto, and Sally MacIntyre headed out of the dining room. Fred, Velma, and Daphne followed them into the Great Hall.

As everyone was passing through the Great Hall, they heard knocking come from an enormous trunk. Everyone froze.

"Help!" came a voice from inside.

Fred, Velma, and Daphne looked at one another. It wasn't Clift's voice. They ran over to the trunk and opened it.

"Chives?" Sonny DiPesto said.

"I was on my way to check the phones when the lights went out," Chives started explaining. As he spoke, he got out of the trunk. "I couldn't see where I was going. I tripped and fell into the trunk. The lid slammed closed and got stuck."

Mayor Redding said, "Thank goodness that ghost didn't get you, too." She turned to Fred, Daphne, and Velma. "I think we can all  squeeze into my car. Would you like a ride to town?"

"No, thanks," Fred answered. "We, uh, have to, uh —"

"Find our friends," Daphne interrupted.

"I wouldn't stay too long," Sally MacIntyre warned. "In Scotland, we take our ghosts very seriously. I advise you to do the same."

"We'll be fine," Velma assured them.

"Well, I'll be sure to send a tow truck, then," Mayor Redding said. "Good night." She, Sonny, and Sally started down the huge staircase.

Chives turned to Fred, Daphne, and Velma. "You should listen to Ms. MacIntyre and leave this place," he warned. "I've lived here for years. That ghost means business. I'm not going to let what happened to Master Clift happen to me." Chives turned and hurried down the stairs. A moment later, the front door slammed shut.

Shaggy and Scooby then joined Fred, Daphne, and Velma in the Great Hall. They both still had napkins tied around their necks.

"Like, where did everyone go?" Shaggy asked.

"They went to get help," Daphne said.

"Sounds like a good plan to me," Shaggy suggested.

"I have a better idea," Fred said.

Velma nodded in agreement. "Let's get to the bottom of this."

"I was afraid you were going to say that," Shaggy moaned.

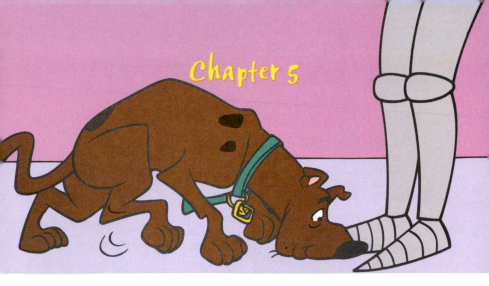

Chapter 5

"Let's split up, gang," Fred said. "Velma, you, Shaggy, and Scooby look around here in the Great Hall. Daphne and I will check out the dining room."

"Like, Scooby and I could check out the dining room while you three look around here," Shaggy volunteered.

Scooby nodded his head in agreement. "Reah, reah, reah."

"Come on, you two," Velma said. "The quicker we get started the quicker we can finish." Fred and Daphne went back into the dining room. Velma pointed toward the suits of armor. "You two look over there. I'll look around here."

Shaggy and Scooby walked over to one of the suits of armor.

"Like, how'd anybody get out of these things?" Shaggy asked.

"Ran ropener!" Scooby said.

"Can opener? That's funny, Scooby-Doo!" The two of them laughed.

Across the room, Velma was looking at the weapons hanging on the wall. She reached up and touched a giant shield. In the middle of the shield was a lion. It was made of solid gold with large emerald eyes. The teeth were made of silver, and its front paw was raised to attack.

"Must be the Montgomery family crest," she said to herself. Velma traced the design of the lion with her hand. Then she noticed something. The lion's claws were made of silver and stuck out from the shield. Velma touched the claws. Suddenly, a doorway

30

opened in the middle of the stone wall.

"Jinkies," she whispered to herself. "It's a secret passage." She took a flashlight from

her pocket. She turned it on and went into the passage. The secret door closed behind her.

Meanwhile, Shaggy was putting on one of the metal helmets. He picked up a sword and posed like a knight. "Hey, look at me, Scooby. I'm Sir Loin of Beef! Get it? Sir Loin? Sirloin?" He and Scooby laughed. "You can be Sir Scoobalot."

"Scooby-Dooby-Doobalot!" Scooby sang.

"And we must duel to the death for the last piece of roast beef," Shaggy added. "Take that!" Shaggy yelled. Shaggy lunged at Scooby and Scooby ducked. Scooby grabbed a sword from one of the knights. He lunged at Shaggy, but Shaggy jumped back and ran after Scooby.

"Ruh-roh," Scooby said. He giggled as he weaved around the suits of armor.

"I'll get you, Sir Scoobalot!" Shaggy called as he chased Scooby around the knights. When he finally cornered Scooby, Shaggy said, "And now, Sir Scoobalot, say your prayers!"

Scooby looked up and saw the ghost of Ward Montgomery standing behind Shaggy.

"Rikes! The rhost! The rhost!" Scooby warned.

"That's right, Sir Scoobalot," Shaggy said. "This is about the roast. And the last piece of the roast is mine. So, what do you have to say about that?"

"Rerind rou!"

"The roast is behind me?" Shaggy said. Scooby nodded quickly. Shaggy slowly turned around and looked over his shoulder. He saw the ghost. "Yikes!" he yelled.

"The rhost! The rhost!" both he and Scooby screamed.

Shaggy and Scooby ran through the ghost's legs. "This way, Scoob!" Shaggy called. He ran around and around the suits of armor. Scooby followed. So did the ghost. "Faster, Scooby!" Shaggy and Scooby ducked behind the last suit of armor.

The ghost of Ward Montgomery stood in the middle of the hall. He couldn't see Shaggy and Scooby.

"You know, Scoob," Shaggy panted, "that ghost is more out of breath than we are!"

Scooby tried to get a better look at the ghost. As he peeked his head around, he accidentally hit the suit of armor. With a creak, it slowly fell over onto the suit of armor next to it.

CRASH!

And then — *CRASH! CRASH! CRASH! CRASH! CRASH! CRASH! CRASH! CRASH!* All the suits of armor fell, one after the other, like dominoes. The ghost whipped around and saw Scooby and Shaggy.

"Quick, Scooby-Doo — in here!" Shaggy jumped into the trunk behind them. Scooby followed and slammed the lid.

The ghost ran over to the trunk and locked it.

"I don't like the sound of that," Shaggy said.

"Help!" Shaggy shouted.

"Relp!" Scooby shouted. They pounded on the trunk.

"Help! Velma! Fred! Daphne! Anyone!"

Chapter 6

Scooby and Shaggy were still smushed in the trunk. "I guess we're goners," said Shaggy. "The ghost must've gotten Velma, Fred, and Daphne by now. I told them this place was bad news."

Suddenly, they heard footsteps.

"Oh, no, it's the ghost!" Shaggy exclaimed. "Good-bye, Scooby-Doo."

"Rood-rye, Raggy."

They heard a click. They shut their eyes. The lid opened, and Shaggy cracked open his right eye just a bit.

"Fred! Daphne! Boy, are we glad to see you!"

The two of them jumped out of the trunk. Shaggy hugged Fred. Scooby hugged Daphne. Shaggy hugged Daphne. Scooby hugged Fred. Shaggy hugged Scooby.

"Knock it off, you two," Fred said sternly. "Have you seen Velma?"

"Like, we thought she was with you," Shaggy answered.

"And we thought she was still with you," Daphne replied.

"This is getting real creepy, man," Shaggy said. "First Clift and now Velma. Like, I told you this place was bad news."

"Rad news!" Scooby echoed.

"Hey! Where is everybody?" It was Velma's voice. And it was coming from the dining room.

The gang ran into the dining room. There was Velma, sitting in Clift's seat at the head of the table.

"There you are," she said.

"Are you all right?" Daphne asked.

"Jinkies," Velma replied. "I'm great. And I found some things that will help us solve this mystery."

"Like, like what?" asked Shaggy.

"For starters, wouldn't you like to know where I've been?" Velma asked.

"We were just trying to figure that out," Fred said.

"While Shaggy and Scooby were playing

knights of the kitchen table," Velma recounted, "I was on the other side of the Great Hall. I noticed the Montgomery family shield on the wall. I discovered a switch that opened a hidden door."

"A secret passage!" Fred exclaimed.

"Not just one," Velma added. "A whole bunch of secret walkways. They go all over the castle."

"Walkways that make it easy for a ghost to get around quickly," Daphne added.

"But only if the ghost knows his way around," Velma replied.

"I'll tell you one thing about that ghost," Shaggy said. "He may be able to get around quickly, but he's a little out of shape."

"What are you talking about, Shaggy?" Daphne asked.

"I've never seen a ghost out of breath before," Shaggy replied.

Velma and Fred looked at each other and nodded.

"I've got a good idea just who our ghost really is," Velma said.

"If you're thinking what I'm thinking," Fred said, "it's time to set a trap."

40

Chapter 7

The gang huddled together at the head of the dinner table. "Okay, everyone, listen up. Here's the plan," Fred began. "We know we have a ghost who wants everyone out of the castle. But why?"

"So he can eat all this food himself?" Shaggy suggested. Shaggy looked at the dinner table still set for dinner.

"Actually, Shaggy, you're not that far off," Velma replied. "There's clearly something in this castle that the ghost wants for himself."

"Right," Fred said. "So we're going to get this ghost to show himself by pretending we're not going anywhere. But that won't be enough, so we'll have to scare him. So, how do you scare a ghost?"

"Sneak up behind him and yell, 'Boo!' " Daphne said.

"Exactly," Velma replied.

"But where are we going to get another ghost?" Shaggy asked.

Everyone then turned to Scooby.

"Ruh?" Scooby said.

"Come on, Scooby-Doo, there's nothing to it," Fred said. "We'll dress you up. All you'll have to do is say 'Boo' when the ghost appears."

"Ruh-uh," Scooby said, shaking his head.

"Please, Scooby?" Daphne asked.

"Roh way." He sat down and crossed his paws.

"Not even for a Scooby snack?" Velma asked.

Scooby did not even blink. "Nope."

"Not even for two Scooby snacks?"

Scooby's stomach growled at the mention of two Scooby snacks. His right ear twitched a little. But he sat firm. "Ruh-ruh."

"Not even for three Scooby snacks?" Velma tried again.

Scooby could not take it any longer. He jumped up and nodded eagerly. "Rokay, rokay, rokay!"

Velma took three Scooby snacks out of her pocket. She threw them to Scooby one at a time.

"Daphne, you and Velma sit at the table

and pretend to be eating dinner," Fred said.

"Like, why can't I sit at the table and pretend to be eating?" Shaggy asked. "I'm much better at eating than catching ghosts."

"Shaggy, you help Scooby get into his costume. Then stand over there behind the grandfather clock. Scooby will hide behind this curtain and I'll be next to him. When Scooby scares the ghost, grab the tablecloth. I'll help you capture the ghost."

"If you say so," Shaggy said. He helped Scooby into some pieces of armor. Daphne and Velma took their places at the dinner table. Scooby hid behind a curtain hanging on the wall. Fred stood in front of the curtain. Shaggy stood next to the grandfather clock on the opposite wall.

"Boy, am I glad we decided to stay through the night," Daphne said.

"Yeah," Velma added. "No ghost is going to scare me."

"Especially one as harmless as Ward

Montgomery," Daphne said loudly.

They started to help themselves to some food. Suddenly, the lights went out. When they came back on, the ghost of Ward Montgomery was there.

"I warned you people to leave before midnight. Now it is too late. This castle and everyone in it are cursed for all time."

Fred looked over at Scooby and nodded.

Scooby gulped and cleared his throat. He jumped out from behind the curtain. "Scooby-Dooby-BOOOOOOOOO!" he yelled.

The ghost turned around. He saw Scooby and leaped back.

"Now, Shaggy!" Fred yelled.

Shaggy jumped out from his hiding place. He grabbed the tablecloth from the large table and gave it a quick tug. *Whoosh!*

The giant cloth flew out from under the plates. He and Fred threw it over the ghost. Daphne and Velma pushed the ghost down into a chair.

"You are all cursed!" the ghost yelled from under the tablecloth.

The next thing they heard was pounding

coming from behind the walls.

"Yikes! It's the real ghost!" Shaggy yelled.

Scooby-Doo jumped out of his armor and dived under the table.

"So much for can openers, eh, Scoob?" Shaggy said. "Save some space for me!" He dived under the table after Scooby.

Chapter 8

"Don't be silly," Velma said. "There is no ghost!" She walked up to the grandfather clock. She ran her fingers over the clock until she found something. Then she pushed a button and a doorway opened. Out came Clifton Montgomery. His hands were tied. There was tape on his mouth. He had a bump on his forehead. But aside from all that, he was fine.

"Clift!" Daphne said. "Are you all right?" She slowly removed the tape from his mouth.

48

"Frightfully woozy, but otherwise fine, thanks," he said.

Fred kept an eye on the ghost while Velma and Daphne untied Clift. Clift sat down and gently felt his forehead.

"Jinkies, what a bump," Velma said.

"Yes, indeed," Clift said. He reached for a glass of water.

"Do you remember what happened?" Velma asked.

"I remember telling everyone the news about the castle. And the lights went out and the ghost of my great-great-grandfather ap-  peared. Next thing I know, I'm tucked away in a tiny little closet somewhere."

Daphne pointed under the table. "Speaking of being tucked away," she said.

"Shaggy. Scooby. You can come out now," Velma said. "It was only Clift."

Shaggy and Scooby popped right up.

"Like, we knew that. We were just, uh —"

"Making sure the floor was all right?" Daphne asked.

All of a sudden, there was another strange knock. Everyone froze.

"Not another ghost," Shaggy moaned.

"No, just the front door," Clift said.

They heard the door open and voices in the hallway.

"Hello? Anyone here?"

"In here," Clift called.

Mayor Redding entered the room with some policemen.

"Clift! Thank goodness you're all right. I'm sorry it took so long, but the storm caused some trouble on the roads."

"How about we see if this ghost is who we think it is?" Fred asked.

"Great idea," Clift agreed.

Fred took the tablecloth off the ghost's head. "Would you like to do the honors, Clift?" Fred asked.

"Love to." Clift lifted off the ghost's mask.

Clift gasped. "Chives!" Clift shouted. "But why?"

Chives looked sadly at Clift. "Because, sir, this is my home. I wanted to scare everyone off so that I wouldn't have to leave. I've been here most of my life. And unlike you, sir, I don't have summer homes and other places to live. Without Montgomery Castle, I'd be a man without a home." A tear filled his eye.

"Oh, Clift," Mayor Redding said, "you really can't blame dear old Chives. You don't have to press charges, do you?"

Velma stepped up. "Excuse me, Mr. Montgomery," she said, "but before you make any decisions, maybe you should ask Chives about the treasure."

"Treasure?" Shaggy asked.

"Yes, the Montgomery family treasure," Clift responded. "But how did you know about it?"

"I did some exploring through the secret passageways," Velma said.

"Good show, Velma," Clift said. "And I guess you found the family treasure chest."

"I did," Velma answered proudly.

"Well, Chives, what do you have to say for yourself now?" Clift asked.

Chives looked up at the cops and then at Clift.

"It's true. I wanted the Montgomery treasure. I figured it was the least you could do for me after all these years of service to your family. I didn't care what happened to this drafty, cold dungeon of a home. I just needed enough time to get the treasure chest packed away so I could leave the country."

Clift turned to Fred, Daphne, and Velma. "Why did you suspect Chives?" he asked.

Fred spoke first. "At first we suspected Mr. DiPesto. When the lights came back on, he was holding the ghost's candle."

"But he couldn't have done it," Daphne added. "He was sitting next to me the whole time."

"It was after we found Chives in the trunk that things first started coming together," Velma said. "He told us he tripped in the darkness and got locked in the trunk. A perfect alibi."

"But the trunk is in the Great Hall," Fred continued. "And that room is lit by candles, not electricity. When the lights went out in the dining room, the candles stayed lit in the Great Hall. Chives was the only one not with us when the ghost appeared."

"He's also lived here a long time," Daphne added. "And probably knows his way around the secret passages."

"But it was Shaggy and Scooby who confirmed it," Velma said. "After the ghost chased them around the Great Hall, they said the ghost was out of breath."

"Real ghosts don't get tired out," Fred explained. "But old men do."

Chives looked up at them. "I would have gotten away with it if it weren't for those kids and their pesky dog."

"Take this man away, officers," Mayor Redding said. "The tow truck will be here soon," she said to the gang. "They're a little backed up because of the weather. Thank you all for helping Clift and solving this mystery. Good-bye, Clift, and thank you again for your generous gift. I'll have my office call you in the morning."

"You're welcome, Mayor. It's my pleasure."

The mayor left with the police officers and Chives. Clift turned to the gang.

"I am very grateful to all of you. Until your van is fixed, why don't we go ahead and have that supper?"

"I thought you'd never ask," Shaggy said happily.

"And for you," Clift said to Scooby-Doo, "I have a special treat." Clift walked over to the table. He reached for a silver dome with a small handle on top. He lifted the dome with a flourish. "The last piece of roast beef!" he exclaimed.

"Scooby-Dooby-Doobalot!" Scooby shouted.

Everyone laughed as they sat down to eat.

About the Author

As a boy, James Gelsey used to run home from school to watch the Scooby-Doo cartoons on television (only after finishing his homework). Today, he still enjoys watching them with his wife and daughter. He also has a real dog named Scooby who loves nothing more than a good Scooby Snack!